This Annual belongs to

Age

My favourite engines are

Annual 2015

Contents

EGMONT

We bring stories to life

First published in Great Britain in 2014 by Egmont UK Limited
The Yellow Building, 1 Nicholas Road, London W 11 4AN
Written by Emily Stead. Edited by Jane Riordan. Designed by Suzanne Cooper

Thomas the Tank Engine & Friends™

CREATED BY BRITT ALLCROFT

Based on the Railway Series by the Reverend W Awdry
© 2014 Gullane (Thomas) LLC. A HIT Entertainment company.
Thomas the Tank Engine & Friends and Thomas & Friends are trademarks of Gullane (Thomas) Limited.
Thomas the Tank Engine & Friends and Design is Reg. U.S. Pat. & Tm. Off.

All rights reserved.

ISBN 978 1 4052 7213 1
57520/1
Printed in Italy

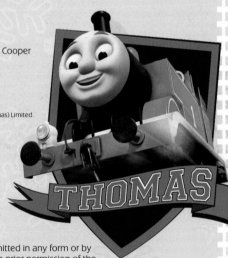

Number 1 Engine

Colour in this picture of Thomas
using the little picture to help you.

Thomas is the
number 1 engine
on Sodor!

All
aboard!

Bust My Buffers!

Who does each pair of buffers belong to?
Follow the trails with your fingers to find out.

1

2

3

Toby

Victor

Gordon

Answers are on page 68.

Millie

love Millie x

Millie is a beautiful blue tank engine who runs on Narrow Gauge rails. Millie lives and works at Ulfstead Castle with her owner, Sir Robert Norramby. Her job is to take visitors on a tour of the Castle in an open-topped carriage!

Best friend: Luke
Fuel: Coal
Paintwork: Blue
Millie loves: Her job pulling passengers around Ulfstead Castle.
Millie doesn't like: Being shut up in her shed.

The Fat Controller's Fact
Millie comes from France. Instead of saying "hello", Millie says, "bonjour" when she sees her friends. Can you say "bonjour"?

Splendid!

Mountain Visit

Thomas is visiting his Narrow Gauge Engine friends at the Blue Mountain Quarry.

Can you find these close-ups in the big picture?
Tick the box as you find each one.

Not Now, Charlie!

This is a story about Charlie, a little engine who loves to make his friends laugh.

Charlie is a playful purple engine. He loves telling jokes!

"What is pink and grey and has four feet?" said Charlie at the Docks one day. "I don't know," said Gordon. "What *is* pink and grey and has four feet?"
"An elephant with its tongue sticking out!" smiled Charlie. Gordon laughed. And Charlie chuffed happily away.

But not everyone likes Charlie's jokes. Sometimes the engines are too busy. "Not now, Charlie!" they say.

One day, Charlie was on his way to pick up some trucks when he had a big surprise.

There, on the tracks, was a great big elephant! Charlie didn't know there were any elephants on Sodor.

"That elephant is in danger. I must do something!" cried Charlie. He blew his whistle as loudly as he could. "PEEP! PEEP!" But the elephant didn't move.

"I must fetch help!" said Charlie.

Charlie puffed round a bend and saw Thomas.
"Stop, Thomas! STOP!" Charlie called out.
"There's an elephant on the line!"

Thomas thought it was another one of Charlie's jokes.
"Not now, Charlie!" he said, grumpily. "Your jokes
are going to make me late." And he steamed away.

When Percy puffed by, he thought Charlie
was joking too. "Not now, Charlie!"
said Percy.

Just then, Charlie spotted a fallen tree on the tracks up ahead. It had knocked down a wall – the wall to the Animal Park!

"The elephant must have escaped!" said Charlie.

Charlie rushed to Brendam Docks to tell everyone about the elephant. But no one believed him. "It's just another one of Charlie's jokes," Thomas sighed.

Charlie sped away feeling silly. He had to find someone who would help him.

Charlie puffed to the Sodor Search and Rescue Centre.
Harold listened to Charlie's tale about the elephant,
and Harold believed Charlie.

"This is an emergency!" Harold buzzed.

At the Animal Park the park keepers were mending
the wall, but the elephant wasn't there.
Charlie and Harold went to search for the elephant.
Before long, Harold spotted it near
the Docks and radioed for help.

The park keepers guided the elephant carefully onto Charlie's special truck. Then Charlie puffed proudly to the Animal Park to take the elephant home.

The Fat Controller was waiting there to meet him. "Well done, Charlie!" he said. "You are a Really Useful Engine."

Charlie beamed. He decided not to tell any more jokes for a while. But, of course, that didn't last long!

Sing-Along

Join in with this song all about the engines,
then try to answer the questions.

They're 2, they're 4, they're 6, they're 8,
Shunting trucks and hauling freight.
Red and green and brown and blue,
They're the Really Useful crew!

All with different roles to play
Round Tidmouth Sheds or far away.
Down the hills and round the bends,
Thomas and his friends.

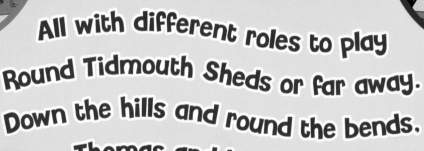

Answers are on page 68.

Thomas, he's the cheeky one,
James is vain but lots of fun.
Percy pulls the mail on time,
Gordon thunders down the line.
Emily really knows her stuff,
Henry toots and huffs and puffs,
Edward wants to help and share,
Toby, well let's say he's square!

The Fat Controller's Questions

1. Who thunders down the line?
2. Who is engine number 6?
3. What is the name of the splendid red engine?
4. Where would you find the engine sheds?
5. Which engine looks square?

Come and join in!

19

Spot the Difference

①

Cinders and ashes!

Thomas has come off the rails.

Colour in a suitcase for each difference you find.

②

These pictures look the same but there are **5** differences in **Picture 2**.

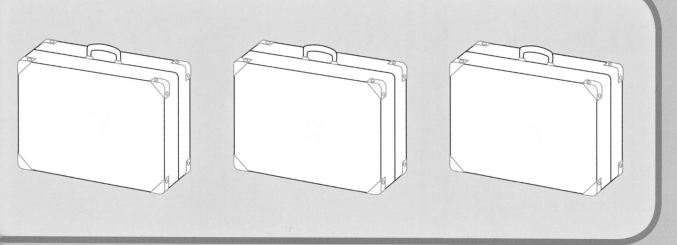

Match the Shadows

The Narrow Gauge Engines on Sodor run on smaller rails. Draw a line to match the little engines to their shadows.

Look carefully at their funnels to tell the engines apart!

1

PETER SAM

a

2

RUSTY

b

3

LUKE

c

4

VICTOR

d

Answers are on page 68.

Norman

love Norman x

Norman may look like his twin, Diesel, but he is a much kinder diesel engine! He works at the Dieselworks and always does as he is told. Poor Norman often breaks down. He would love to be fixed properly so he could be a **Really Useful Engine** all the time.

Best friend: Norman wants to be liked by all the engines – Diesel or Steamies.
Fuel: Diesel
Paintwork: Dark orange
Norman loves: Helping other engines.
Norman doesn't like: Breaking down.

The Fat Controller's Fact

When the turntable at Tidmouth Sheds was frozen, Norman told Thomas he could sleep at the Dieselworks.

Splendid!

Perfect Pieces

Which jigsaw piece is missing from this picture of Thomas and his brave friend, Captain?

1

(a)

(b)

(c)

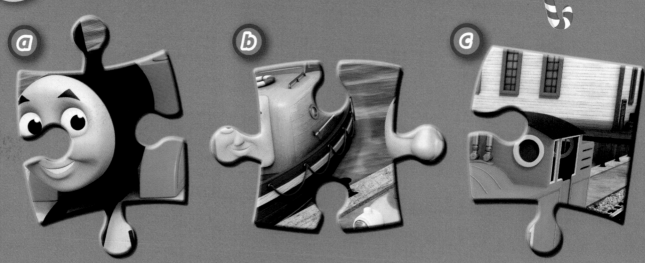

Now try this jigsaw puzzle
of Tale of the Brave hero Gator.

Well done,
good work!

Gordon Runs Dry

Read this story all about Gordon the Big Engine.
When you see a picture, say the word.

Gordon   Paxton   Thomas

signal   water tower

It was a sunny day on Sodor. was hurrying along

with his trucks of stone. Suddenly the turned red

and  had to stop quickly.  was steaming

the other way. "Express coming through!" he boomed.

But a big stone flew out of the diesel engine's

truck and bashed  on his boiler.

 hadn't gone far when his boiler began to run dry.

As Hiro huffed on, the smell of dirty smoke got worse. But there was no time to stop for fresh coal. Hiro was determined to get his job done on time.

When he got to the Docks, The Fat Controller was waiting. "I need you go to the Smelter's Yard to collect some heavy iron girders. Henry will be your back engine."

The Fat Controller didn't know about the bad coal.

Puff! Puff!

At the Smelter's Yard, Henry was surprised to see Hiro. "Did you pull those trucks without fresh coal?" he asked.

"Yes," said Hiro. "It wasn't easy, but sometimes you have to keep on puffing."

And so they did. Heaving and huffing, they set off with the train of heavy iron girders. But as they reached Gordon's Hill, there was a very strange noise.

"My firebox is blocked!" cried Hiro. Hiro had broken down!

"Don't worry, Hiro," smiled Henry. "You taught me to keep on puffing, so that is what I'm going to do."

Henry clunked and clanked. His wheels were wobbly and his axles ached. But he kept on puffing. Slowly they started to move up the hill. Henry was pushing the heavy train and Hiro!

Everyone clapped as Henry puffed into the Docks. "Hooray!" they cheered. Henry was a hero! That night, with fresh coal, Henry and Hiro felt much better.

"You were right, Hiro," smiled Henry. "Sometimes you can keep puffing, even with bad coal."

"But it's much nicer with good clean coal!" Hiro laughed.

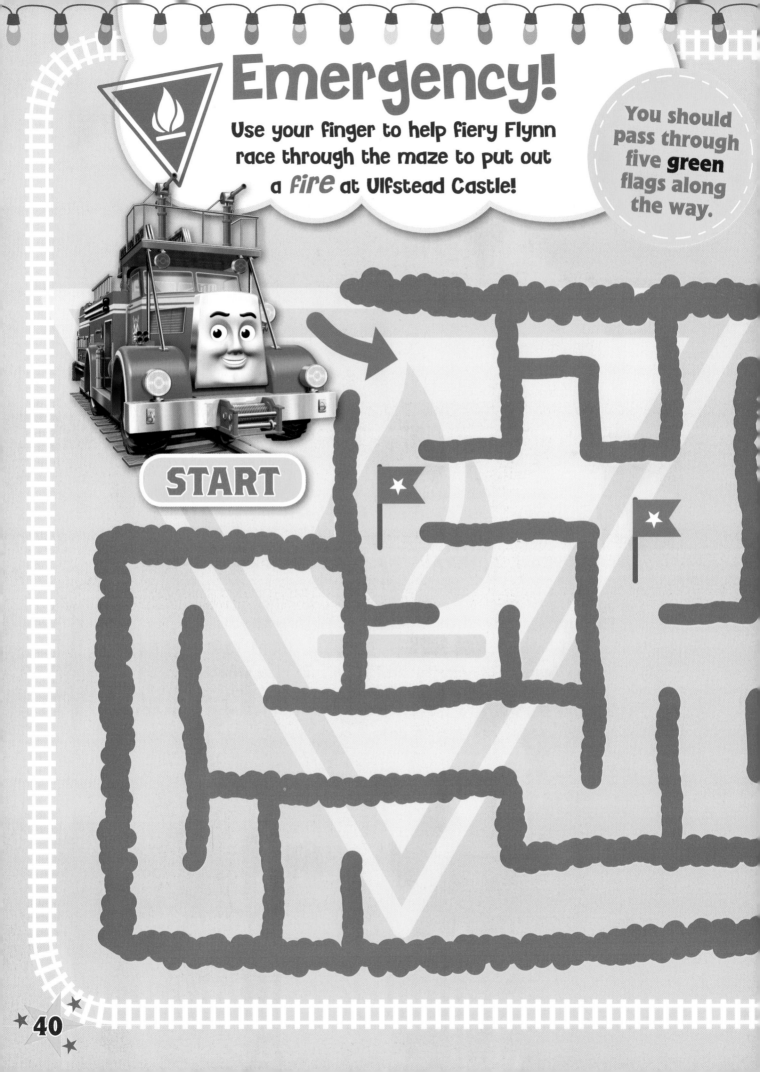

Emergency!

Use your finger to help fiery Flynn race through the maze to put out a *fire* at Ulfstead Castle!

You should pass through five **green** flags along the way.

START

That evening, Harvey the Crane Engine came to get Thomas back on the tracks.

The Fat Controller spoke sternly to Thomas. "You have caused confusion and delay," he said.

Thomas was very sorry. He promised to stay on his branch line and not take any more shortcuts from then on.

But Thomas and Bertie still like to have races, and sometimes Thomas even wins!

Winter Wonderland

Winter is a busy time on the Island of Sodor. The weather is cold and sometimes it snows. The engines must keep chuffing hard so that their axles don't ice up!

The Steamies deliver trucks of coal all over the Island to make sure that everyone can keep warm.

But the trucks aren't always filled with coal!

What do you think is inside these presents?

Really Useful Engines keep puffing whatever the weather!

Which three engines can you see here at Tidmouth Sheds?

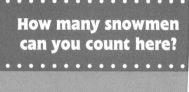

How many snowmen can you count here?

The children on the Island love to build snowmen.

Sometimes the engineers make snowmen too!

Thomas always wears his snowplough when heavy snow has fallen. He learnt his lesson a long time ago when a tractor called Terence had to pull Thomas out of a snowdrift!

What do you think Percy might be thinking?

Poor Percy once ended up funnel-deep in snow too!

Do you like snow?

51

Which engines are out in the snow here?

Winter is some of the engines' favourite time of year . . .

Do you know which number Henry the Green Engine is?

. . . while snow makes other engines' wheels whirr with worry!

Each year, there is a special winter party. The engines **love** to fetch decorations to make the Island look festive.

What shape is the decoration on Thomas' flatbed?

What colours can you see here?

Sometimes the engines are decorated too! Emily loves to light up the Steamworks!

Answers are on page 68.

There is a Christmas tree at each station on Sodor.

Everybody helps to deliver them!

The Christmas trees really do look **splendid!**

And the winter party wouldn't be the same without this very **important guest!**

Have a wonderful winter, everyone!

Who do you think has dressed up as Father Christmas?

Can you guess?

love Winston x

Winston is a car on rails! He works with The Fat Controller, inspecting the tracks on Sodor Railway to see whether they need repairing. He may look funny, but Winston is a kind and thoughtful car who is careful not to get in the way when the engines are at work.

Best friend: The Fat Controller, even though he is a terrible driver!
Fuel: Diesel
Paintwork: Red
Winston loves: His work, inspecting tracks for damage.
Winston doesn't like: Bad driving!

The Fat Controller's Fact
Once Winston was dressed up as Father Christmas' sleigh on Christmas Eve, which he didn't like at all!

Ho! Ho! Ho!

54

Tricky Twins

Draw lines to match
the engine pairs.

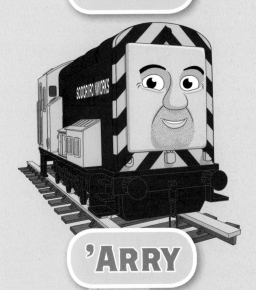

BILL

DASH

'ARRY

BEN

BASH

BERT

Answers are on page 68.

★ **Paxton**

love Paxton x

Paxton, or Pax for short, works at the Blue Mountain Quarry. His job is to carry trucks of slate to other parts of the Island. Paxton has a good heart and Knows right from wrong. He sometimes makes mistakes, but always tries his best.

Best friend: Thomas
Fuel: Diesel
Paintwork: Dark green.
Paxton loves: Steam engines and he works well with the Narrow Gauge Engines too.
Paxton doesn't like: Seeing others in trouble.

The Fat Controller's Fact
Paxton was once buried in rubble when Blondin Bridge collapsed. He was sent to the Dieselworks to be repaired and is now as good as new.

Hurray!

Goodbye!

All the engines in the Steam Team love working on **The Fat Controller's Railway**.

Colour in The Fat Controller, using the coloured dots as a guide. Then say goodbye to his Really Useful Engines.

Goodbye from Thomas and all his friends!

Answers

Page 9 **1 Gordon, 2 Toby, 3 Victor.**

Pages 18–19
1 Gordon, 2 Percy, 3 James, 4 Tidmouth, 5 Toby.

Pages 20–21

Page 22
1 Peter Sam – c, 2 Rusty – d, 3 Luke – a, 4 Victor – b.

Page 24 **Jigsaw piece a is missing.**

Page 25 **Jigsaw piece b is missing.**

Page 30 **Scruff is hiding.**

Pages 40–41

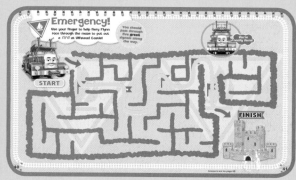

Pages 50–51
The three Really Useful Engines are Thomas, Henry and Emily. There are 6 snowmen.

Pages 52–53
**The engines hidden in the snow are Emily, Thomas and Percy.
Henry is the number 3 green engine.
Thomas' decoration is a star shape.
The colours of Emily's lights are blue, red, yellow and green.
The Fat Controller is dressed up as Father Christmas!**

Page 63
James is a red tender engine, Thomas is a blue tank engine, James is the number 5 Engine, Thomas is the Number 1 Engine.

Page 64 **The odd engine out is picture 3.**

Page 65 **Bill and Ben, 'Arry and Bert, Bash and Dash are pairs.**

Goodbye!